EVEN WHERE YOU ARE: Keep going as you are

Susan R. Garza

Table of content

Same Class

I'm sure I'll murder at some point. I don't understand why professors seldom acknowledge the terrible quality of group work most of the time. But Shun enjoys working on cooperative projects. However, when you aren't allowed to pick your teammates, group projects are embarrassing.

Joining forces with Shuuji Yuuta, the second-quietest and coldest student in my class, wasn't quite in line with my idea for "The Best Group Project Ever." In an attempt to interact with him and start a friendship that had stalled over the last several weeks since he moved here, I went up to him during recess while putting on a false grin.

One of my middle school friends, Shuuji, was a good chef. He used to live close to our house, so when my parents went out for some alone time, my mother would ask him over and he would cook for us. He was also intelligent. After Shun and I, where Shun took first as usual and I came in second with just a little less effort, came third. Shuuji was reserved and always gave the other person silent treatment. Nevertheless, he was well-liked by the females; anybody would be seduced by a face so attractive. Shame he wasn't my style. I'd rather be friends with someone.

"Hey!" I sat down in the vacant chair in front of him after pulling it there, then I turned to face him. He continued reading while casting an angry glance up from his book. What on earth was his issue? We would be working in groups for the next two weeks, so I had the idea that we may get close before we started.

no response

I grimaced. That attitude, what was it? What was going on with this guy?

Shun approached me after noticing my difficulty and asked, "Chikashi, would you mind going with me somewhere?" You wouldn't mind if I borrowed him for a little time, right? He asked Shuuji with a pleasant grin.

"Please get rid of him."

This is such crap.

Despite my objections, Shun hauled me away, telling me, "Don't approach him like that."

"I know." I huffed, obviously irritated. I never had a good reason to keep anything from him.

You are well aware of his personality, but do you care?

When he asked, I simply shrugged, and the bell sounded just in time. He groaned, and I could understand what he was thinking. After that, we both walked back to class while once again dreading science.

We carried on, as usual, the following day, but I'm still trying to get Shuuji to communicate. He instructed Shun to take me away yesterday, which was the first time I've heard him speak in a while. Real frustration exists.

Finally, I agreed with him that if he talked to me, I would leave him alone. Then I mumbled, "for 5 seconds," under my breath, making sure he wouldn't overhear what I was going to say.

What do you want? Shuuji eventually answered after sighing and giving up. Woah... His voice was rather pleasant. It was lovely.

For you to speak I guess I was feeling a little proud of myself.

"I am speaking. What do you desire, then?"

"To better understand you." When I stated that, he went silent again and hid behind the book he was reading. Anyone would have given up by now, yet this motivated me to keep going. Lessons went on and were finished.

The entire school rose nearly simultaneously as the last bell rang, thanked their instructors, and started packing their bags. Shuuji was seated far behind me, so I hurried over to him and smiled at him. What do you need from me, he groaned as he cast a sidelong glance at me.

I held up my patience and said, "We should get started on our endeavor," even though he remained silent for a long time before nodding.

"Visit me at my home. In any case, you never leave right away for home.

How did you find out?

I have a method. I said, cracking a little smile at the faint look of alarm on his face. I was asked to lead the route when Shuuji conceded to my strategies.

The thought of remaining too far away and, let alone, being alone, terrified me when Shun indicated he would remain at school. No... Us. So, Shuuji and I hung around with him for a while.

Shun was the one who spoke to Shuuji on our return trip, and unlike how he treated me, Shuuji answered. Though I was aware that I had no cause to be envious of my twin, Shun's constant assurance occasionally bothered me. He never boasted about it, though. As one could expect from the eldest, huh?

Yumi came out to get us, and I heard her footsteps as she did. Shuuji entered after the two of us. She started junior high this year at the age of 12.

She was also quite well-liked.

Hey guys! Also a vivacious little one, "welcome back!"

After taking off my shoes, I grinned and fluffed her hair, while Shun patted her on the head and said, "I'm home," together. As though he had been in this place for a very long time, Shuuji removed his shoes. Please pardon my interruption.

Yumi smiled at him, her eyes sparkling at the sight of him, and he patted her shoulder, saying, "hello, Yumi." Yumi's grin deepened, and I was very sure she felt successful after hearing someone she hadn't seen in two years shout her name.

As I dropped my suitcase on the couch, I giggled at the sight. "I'll go get myself cleaned up and go down as quickly as possible."

Shuuji nodded, and I rose.

The warmth of the water against my skin was soothing. I cleansed my face and ran my fingers through my hair. Shuuji hasn't been here in a long time, and my room is a disaster since I didn't clean it, and I was hoping he wouldn't come in.

I sighed as I emerged from the restroom with a towel around my waist. What's with the sigh, you ask? I turned away from the voice and moved over to my cabinet when it said, "Nothing."

"Your room is quite disorganized. It appears that nothing has been done to clean it since I stopped dropping by.

I jumped. It was who? When I turned back, the raven head was sitting on my bed with his arms crossed over his chest. His eyes were scanning the room before settling on me.

I turned my back on him and looked away because I felt uneasy. His fingers touched my hair and I heard him shuffle before he spoke, "Your hair's still damp... I'll dry it up for you."

"Get out of my room," I said.

I closed my door right away after pushing him out of my room, so I didn't hear the subsequent thump. What was the issue?

My cheeks became scarlet with shame, and I was fighting to catch my breath. But really, why was I feeling self-conscious? He has before shown up in my room, informed me of minutiae I rarely notice, and then corrected them. He didn't appear to be touchy, but he was—just never around my siblings. Ugh... enough contemplation of him.

"You're finally done?" I asked Shuuji as I got dressed and answered the door. My cheeks began to warm as I nodded. He said, "Your hair's still damp," to which I retorted, "I'll dry it up later."

Shuuji groaned. I was irritated, "Shut up, now! I will!"

I followed behind him as we descended. I appreciated his broad back and shoulders because they made me feel as though "I would protect you." Without a doubt, I admired the man a lot.

"Parents will return later, Chikashi. They are out enjoying a beverage."

I sighed and hoped they wouldn't act. Inappropriate...

I'll prepare dinner. Shuuji was already in the kitchen, wearing an apron, and rummaging through the partially-filled refrigerator as I turned to look at it. Immediately, Shun responded by rushing into the kitchen and ordering Shuuji to take a break because he was our guest. However, the man made no move, and my brother eventually gave up and apologized.

Shun sighed as he left the kitchen, and I was left to observe Shuuji as she worked. After a while, I approached him and peered over his shoulder. He was tall, and I was confident that he had grown significantly in just one year, yet I at least reached his chin. What're you creating? I took a quick look at his face, which was somehow stained a pale blood red. What the heck, oh wait? That was adorable, wasn't it? However, it was brief as he hastily turned aside, "Y-Your favorite..."

Wow... He was quite attentive. And in some ways, cute... After some reflection, I realized that his hair was completely black and quite smooth. He had stunning black eyes and a fair complexion, and just amazing... Okay! I'm done now! Take a breath, Chikashi! That's all there is to it—not he's my type!

I exhaled deeply and gradually became less agitated. As soon as I smelled the delicious scent, Shuuji called out that supper was ready. I got to my feet and headed for the table. Yumi nearly fell as she hurried toward the table before Shuuji held her and said, "Careful." What in the world was that sensation? Screw it, I say. Shun and Yumi took their places, and I took mine. Let's eat, Shuuji said as he sat down.

I exhaled in satisfaction as we quickly came to an end. My favorite cuisine hadn't been eaten in a while, and Shuuji's cooking was exquisite. When his mother questioned him about his plans two years ago, he said that he wanted to be a chef. He still wants to be a chef, right?

Now that Shuuji was glaring at me, I shifted in my seat while asking him, "What are you looking at?"

You still eat sloppy, huh? The raven head moved in closer and touched my cheek. He declared.

Shut up, please. I averted his soft look, which wasn't a glare. Shuuji, do you love my brother? Yumi said as she stared carefully at the other side of us.

Why would you say that? Shuuji nearly gasped for breath. He stepped away from me appearing uneasy, which left me feeling a little letdown. Because my buddy has someone who also loves her, and he does it

with the same loving expression in his eyes! She struck up.
I turned to look at Shuuji sitting next to me and noticed that his face was tinged with crimson; it was that anxious expression once more as he rejected his feelings for me. I decided to lightly tease him while I grinned. Since he was as straight as a rod, it is unthinkable that he could be in love with me.

I put on the best seductive face I could conjure as I came closer to him, my hand holding onto his chair as I gazed into his eyes, my knee resting on the small space on his chair, and my other hand resting on the table to support my body "Shuuji, are you sure you don't love me? You realize how much it makes my heart hurt?"

Upon swallowing, Shuuji's adorable blush became darker. Although it was obvious that he was attempting to turn away, his eyes remained fixed on mine. "You two need to quit fawning." I experienced a slight blow to the head. Yumi is present. Shun dissuaded me from approaching and said in a low voice, "You better watch it, don't overdo it."

It's not like he'll like me anyhow, I thought as I pouted a little but nodded.

Shun only sighed.

He won't, I assume.

What The F*ck Just Took Place?

The two geniuses on our team significantly accelerated our project. Our two-week assignment was completed in three days instead. But since my parents were also busy, Shuuji had to keep dropping over and cooking dinner for us the last three nights.

We completed the entire assignment quickly and accurately, and when I brought it to our instructor, she simply waved her hand and nodded at us. I glanced at Shuuji, who gave me a shrug, and we both left the staff room.

We're finally done, right?

I don't know why, but as Shuuji shrugged, he had his attention focused on the route in front of him rather than on me. I turned around when I heard my name and saw two of our female classmates waving at me. I smiled and waved back, stopping in my tracks, and to my surprise, Shuuji slowed down to a halt a little in front of me.

"I've heard that your project is already complete, Chikashi-kun! Can you assist us with ours?"

Her eyes were on Shuuji as she spoke to me while twirling a hair strand around her finger. What a flirt, I see. She was pretty much the nastiest girl in the entire classroom, and I recognized her. A few days ago, I accidentally bumped into her; I apologized, but even then, she yelled at me and laid responsibility on me. Doesn't sound so horrible, does it? When the teacher came, she adopted a victim role.

Even after realizing that she was trying to flirt, Shuuji remained unfazed at all. He declined to flirt back. I couldn't help but smile a little bit. My mouth was open to the object. She was bothersome, it was our work, and we should do them ourselves, thus I didn't like her.

"No." As soon as I spoke, Shuuji grabbed my wrist and hauled me away.

Wow, he appeared angry because of how tightly he was holding my wrist. Just picture him pinning me with it, all right, cut. Not what I ought to be considering. Shuuji, we're currently a long way from them.

He started to slow down and then stopped. What was it that honestly made me uncomfortable now? Was he fond of her? Did he not want me to approach her closely?

"Sorry." He offered an apology before leaving.

What...?

Why the heck

"Hey!"

The next time I saw him in class, he was quiet and wouldn't even look my way.

He was behaving strangely. Every time he spotted me, he would turn away. Stay away from me. This persisted for a few days. Not that I mind,

Well, I did mind.

What was the issue? acting so touching, affectionate, and near to me yet ignoring me! Lord help me! Just when I was beginning to feel like I was getting to know him better... I'm unable to comprehend his thoughts, and that aggravates me.

As I lay on my bed, I grasped the blanket in my hands. I yelled into my pillow before exhaling deeply and feeling better.

Why was I so concerned? 3 days to experience something unique? Fuck this nonsense.

I left the next day because it was the weekend. The number of people of my sort that wander the streets would astound one.

Although I didn't need to keep anything from my family, I didn't give the whole story. I didn't feel I needed to. They wouldn't mind if I returned their calls, though. Nevertheless, because Shun asked, I told him.

I sighed in frustration as I tried to find someone because my thoughts were focused on you, Shuuji. I inhale deeply as I pat my cheeks. Okay, let's stop procrastinating and start looking for someone. Particularly those close to my age were all in a frantic and confused state.

xxxxxx

And I did discover one... But it's more like he discovered me.

Oh my, I feel like I've just gotten caught in a trap.

In a dim alleyway, his hands were placed close to my head on the wall. His eyes had the appearance of a wolf that had discovered a little meal. Since he kept it carefully hidden from everyone and because he was a member of the student government, it came as a surprise and a major shock. Senji Kurokawa is a notorious pervert and womanizer.

Did he make a double move?

Oikawa Chikashi, am I correct?

Surprisingly, He could distinguish between my brother and me.

He clicked his tongue, evidently indignant, "I've had my sights on you for some time now, damn bastard didn't allow me to get near to you."

However, the irritation only persisted for a little while before being quickly replaced with pride and intrigue. He pulled me in closer while holding my waist and said in my ear, "You are now mine. You must date me; there is no other option."

He let go, fluffed my hair, and walked away while giggling.

My ears were warmer than the sun, and my cheeks were hot and burning. Oh my God, if I had lost my senses, I would have been on fire.

That vice president is a bum. Damn that womanizer—ugh, damn that.

Screw This, I'm leaving.

The day before was just as awful as yesterday. After "confessing," the Kurokawa bastard decided to go see my parents to "make it official."

My mother asked me to open the door after hearing the doorbell ring because it was her time to do the washing. Yes, we all did it in shifts, even dad.

What are you doing in this place?

"Visiting."

Who's there, Chikashi? I could hear my mother calling out to me. Kurosawa, I tightened my teeth and drew him up to my eye level, saying, "Don't you dare do something dumb." I cautioned him before releasing my grip.

Will you please hold me closer once more? The expression on his face had changed from astonished to amused.

My complexion darkened. I had to completely control my flushing in his presence. He removed his shoes and set them to the side, saying, "Sorry for invading!" as if he had been here for a very long time. He spoke.

Shun strode past the sofa to our right and down the stairs to our left "Vice-President, ah! Is there a problem?" He looked at me and inquired, but after seeing the look on my face, he quickly erased the notion.

"No. Please let me visit your folks." I sighed inaudibly as he looked about, saying, "The moan would sound better under me in bed."

I gasped and punched him hard "Exactly what are you talking about? Fuck you." I get up.

With a little smile on his lips, he laughed.

Ba-dump.

What in the world? When he grins, he looks wonderful...

What brings a nice person like you here, Mum asked as she emerged from the kitchen. As she asked, using the hand towel to dry her hands. "Ah, could I ask if you're Chikashi's sister, you look just identical," Kurokawa said with a smile as he turned to face her.

Why the heck were they using such formal language and flattery? So even if my mother is attractive, he shouldn't compliment her.

I'm their mother, my mother chuckled, looking at me. Did my sweetheart make a mistake?

Kurokawa grimaced and said, "I am sorry. No. I'd want to formally request Chikashi's hand."

I became motionless. my hand Why did he use my hand for what? Whatever did my hand do to him? Don't cut it off, please.

"Hand?"

"I want to date him," she said.

I gasped for air when I heard a couple of thumps, and as I turned to look in the direction of the sound, I saw my father gripping the stair rail. Oh my God... This would be a lengthy day.

Kurokawa and I were seated across from Mom and Dad. When Shun brought us some drinks, Dad had a scowl on his face and was drinking his water quickly. You want to date our Chikashi, right? Mum enquired, her expression showing worry, but she didn't appear to bother.

"Yes."

Dad added, more as a statement than a question, "And you're the vice president."

Mum sighed, "I don't know why I should oppose," "Chikashi?" She glared at me and prompted me to express my acceptance or opposition.

"Wow, what? Mum! I hardly even know him!"

Well, it's an issue between you two," Mum said with a smile as she looked at Kurokawa and I began to unwind.

But, mom! "I'd rather go out with Shuuji than him," I whimpered, feeling rather upset with myself for the whimper. I paused and remembered what I had just said. Yumi cried, Dad coughed, and Shun made jokes. The unfathomable 50 hues of crimson on my cheeks caused me to say, "Th-That... I-I... I just..." Oh my goodness, it nearly sounded like I was confessing, and not explicitly.

"Shuuji...?" Kurokawa spoke in a plain, chilly tone. However, venomous, riven with toxic resentment, "Do you refer to Shuuji Yuuta? How can he help?"

He can prepare delectable meals! But naturally, that one has to be canceled out by my brain, which is why I stammer.

Okay, if you don't mind, lads. Why don't you two discuss this in Chikashi's room? Mum coughed to get our attention.

My spine tingled, and. I'm alone with him in my room. The worst-case scenario is when he is visibly envious and can do anything.

I would not object. Kurokawa grinned, and it served as the cue for me to stop appreciating my entire life. It was brief but Oh, come on, I'm kidding. My brief life was terrible.

Knowing I had no option but to comply with my mother's request, I led the way up. Shun arrived after I sent a "help me" gaze in his direction. Since his room was only next to mine, he feigned to enter it, but I was very sure he was watching out for me.

And you had to come all the way here, I thought as I sat on the side of my bed with my face in my hands.

"Your folks appear to be handling it very well,"

They're aware. A pause

I'll be honest and say I'm not interested in you. Added I

Kurokawa gave me a puppy-dog smile as he glanced at me and then ran his fingers through his blond hair. He was half, so it wasn't a surprise to me that he was blonde. It doesn't matter if you're interested in me or not, he later said after gathering himself. All I want is you.

He approached me by taking a few steps and then leaned forward, his weight supported by his two hands close to me. I was astonished to see how near we were when I looked up. His eyes were hard, stern, and cold. I swallowed. Why someone like him would desire me is beyond me. the way anyone would desire me. As I pulled him away from me, I felt his face on mine. "Stop being so relentless. It's irritating.

Kurokawa remained silent at this time, and I felt his hot breath on the back of my neck as my two wrists were restrained above my head and my head was placed on the comfortable bed.

Whoa, Hey!

I had a hard time moving my hands, and attempted to elude his hold, but he was powerful. My legs were free but my head was worthless. I kicked with all of my might, "Damn this bastard!" He also held them in a position somehow.

When he muttered, "Shh... You wouldn't want your folks to hear you, would you?" I could hear the sneer in his voice.

Oh, I would for sure.

I didn't scream or make a noise, though, since I was afraid he would kiss me anyhow if I did.

I shivered as his breath came close to my ears. I'm breathing more heavily.

In hopes of spotting Shuuji, I peered in the direction of the door as it swung open. I caught sight of him, his pale face fixed on us. He had no one behind him.

Who do I hope to see again?

With horror on his face, Shuuji stood there.

What do you want? Kurokawa growled as he sent a glare his way. Can't you tell we're having a private moment here?

I noticed Shuuji tensing up. I could have explained my sexual orientation to him with a wink if he had been a regular buddy standing there. But the reason was that he wasn't your typical friend. He was...

Kurokawa was dragged away by Shuuji when she seized him by the collar. Their heights were about identical, although Shuuji was a few centimeters higher. His penetrating, evil-looking stare was black.

When the raven lad shoved him away, Kurokawa stumbled backward and groaned.

What a surprise, I must say. Coming to the rescue is Shuuji.

At this point, Shuuji was in front of me, his broad back acting as a shield against me. His big shoulders caught my attention; had they always been this wide? I was holding a tiny piece of his clothing. Perhaps the timing was terrible. I always had poor timing, though.

I exhaled and said, "Shuu."

My head was touched by Shuuji's hand as his back muscles relaxed. "Are you alright?" He muttered.

"Yeah."

Then he nodded, appearing to be somewhat relieved in my opinion.

Kurokawa scowled, "Stop getting in the way. I don't sure why, but the unexpected pun made me want to laugh and restrain myself.

"I'm not. Put a distance between us. Shuuji hissed.

He's not in between, though, I reasoned.

I suddenly felt relieved and yelled "Shun" as I dashed for the door. He turned and had his back to me before I encircled him since I knew he could be seen from the entrance, as I had anticipated. A few drops of water spilled onto the floor when the water cups tipped. The yelling started then, and we could hear it.

"Muuum!! Water on the stairs? Avoid it!

At the foot of the stairs, Yumi was on my right and yelled in my mother's direction.

Oh my God...

"Shun!"

Shun gritted his teeth and said, "For the love of Chikashi, dang it, Mi-chan!" The water then spilled across my shirt as he pushed it in my way and into my palms. "Shun!"

Screw you, I say. He spoke to me in a whisper-shouted tone while smiling slightly.

I giggle, temporarily forgetting what was happening in my chamber.

When I looked back, Shuuji was scowling, "Take off your clothes."

"Hmm? Why?"

He just approached me and pulled my shirt over my head before pausing and bringing it down. He coughed as he turned to face Kurokawa. Kurokawa shrugged and turned around quite reluctantly.

My shirt was dragged over my head by Shuuji, who then tossed it to the side. I trembled when a chilling air touched my chest. The raven lad slung a towel over my shoulder and put on another shirt after removing it from my closet.

After a period of silence and muffled laughter from the door, Shun was seen clinging to the side door with his hand resting on his stomach "Oh, my God! Oh, my God! INSANE shits! What in the world?"

I felt my cheeks start to flush as Shun started laughing, so I grabbed Shuuji's wrist and pulled his hands away from my waist. Shun patted my shoulder and laughed "You've got a lot on your plate. And most likely your mouth shortly." Despite his comments being meant towards me, he started while winking at Shuuji. I caught sight of the raven's head. His cheeks had a deep flush, and f*cckkk...

Kurokawa was dragged from my room by Shun, who approached him and joined their arms. "Alright! It's time to mend your hurt feelings! He said as I heard. Kurokawa switched his attention to me, and I did likewise. He groaned, rubbed his head, grinned at me, and then eagerly followed my brother.

Shuuji sat on my bed, and I was sitting on the floor.

I felt remorseful. Why, though? Why was I remorseful? There was nothing I needed to feel sorry about! It's not like we're in a relationship or that he likes me!

Even if I did like him, he doesn't like me.

But wait a minute... I did, however, apologize to him.

"I'm certain he shoved me down,"

Silence.

Silence...

"Will you say something?"

"Why are you saying sorry?"

"I have no idea!" I was so angry that I tossed the towel I had previously used at him. What a jerk!

It was seized by Shuuji, who then pulled me in close and buried his face in my chest while encircling my waist. "I'm happy," He murmured to me.

I stroked his smooth hair with my fingertips.

Friends. We were only pals. Regardless of how close we were, we could only be friends.

Only here would and could we remain.

Hopefully another typical day.

The comfortable feeling of the well-known cloth on Chikashi's skin led him to adjust his outfit. He observed the person in the mirror as they stood there, their mouth, and the unruly brownish hair that reminded him of his father. He squinted.

He looked good, of course. Shun, his elder twin, is another who has the same characteristics. He sprang out of bed, grabbed his stuff for school, and bounded down the stairs. Shun had gone out the night before with Kurokawa, a womanizer who swung both ways, but not very far because there were no symptoms of discomfort. However, Chikashi couldn't help but think of one specific man.

The man had black hair that reached his shoulder; it was extremely dark, devoid of any brown hairs, and black like a raven's feather. It was confusingly straight yet not exactly straight. He was chilly, and his eyes were frigid. Pun- but occasionally his demeanor didn't match his appearance. He would appear to be staring, but he would be thinking about a stuffed animal or his favorite meal.

Chikashi sat at the table, delighted that it was only he who could distinguish the several facial expressions on the raven head. He described it as a unique gift.

Their mother was facing away from them as his brother ran down the stairs to welcome her. The majority of her hair, which was pulled back into a bun and just a few gray streaks covered her head, was still in good health. She turned around and greeted the children, once more bringing to Chikashi's attention her attractiveness. Being able to truly see his mother with his own two eyes that morning was weird for him. His brother and he had the same likely thought as they locked eyes, "morning old lady."

She grumbled and stopped, "Breakfast will be made by the two themselves while the elderly woman continues to sleep." Your highness, we're joking.

She grinned and concluded by setting the two dishes in front of them. "Of course you were," she said.

"I'm grateful,"

They heard light footsteps, and their mother greeted the person coming down "Hello, Yumi. your footwear" Before even turning to face the brunette, she spoke.

Coughing, Yumi said, "about that..."

"I cleaned it when I noticed it. I owe you one." To his sister, whose eyes were filled with grief, Shun muttered. Yumi, who is 12 years old, muttered angrily before rushing off to retrieve them.

Chikashi rose after finishing the final bite and thanked his mother for the meal. Who is dad?

His mother shrugged, beginning to count down from 10. Shun cleaned the plates at the sink while standing up. "1."

Tooru was tripping as he clung to his suit and tie, which were fluttering about his neck. "Late. Late. Late-!!"

His wife put the prepared food in his eager mouth and said, "As usual." While his wife fastened the tie around his neck, he began to chew.

"That's great. Much love." With his voice muffled by the food in his mouth, Tooru spoke. She gave him one more kiss on the cheek before directing the four of them outside, saying, "Go, go."

Shun bid her farewell as he boarded the car with his shoes on properly as the other two argued over who should sit in front. played a game of rock-paper-scissors to get the answer. Yumi slammed the door shut after entering the front passenger seat and laughing in Chikashi's face.

Their mother chuckled and waved them off as Chikashi complained and got inside the car, locking the door as well.

Chikashi leaned against the door as the well-known trees and buildings rolled by like a movie. His thoughts were now wandering to yesterday's occurrence. His right hand was on his lap in a ball-shaped grip, and he had furrowed brows above his eyes. What was he meant to do at this point?

Shun gave his brother a gentle slap on the back and assured him that he understood and would assist. They didn't take long to go to school after Chikashi found solace in this.

First, to wave, Shun said that he had to look for someone in particular. He mumbled. They were OK as long as they were in the same building, Chikashi chuckled as he walked to class. They felt a little pain, but nothing too uncomfortable.

Shuuji walked up to Chikashi's table, murmuring something. He turned to head back to his seat, appearing satisfied. Why are you doing that?

It would be more accurate to say that Chikashi was always behind him, wondering what the youngster was doing but doing nothing to stop him. "N-nothing," sputtered Shuuji as she began to shiver.

Is that true? Chikashi cocked a brow.

"Yes."

"Kay..." Nevertheless, it sounded more like a query.

Shuuji's heartbeat accelerated. Without a doubt, Chikashi was adorable, and the raven head was madly in love with him. For him, not his identical twin. He was wonderful and priceless.

"Chikashi...?"

The brunette remained seated while entirely pausing his activities to pay attention. "Yes?"

"I enjoy..."

What do you enjoy? Peanuts?"

"No," he said, shaking his head, "I mean yes." But that's not what I was going to say, Chikashi said, his expression showing a hint of amusement.

"Mhmm?"

Why was this so hard? He merely mutters the words "I like you," which Chikashi and Chikashi alone could make out well enough.

The scene before Chikashi caused his heart to race. With his hands in his pockets and his hair still rather long, Shuuji was undoubtedly blushing. Chikashi was forced to look at his eyes, which matched the color of his hair, as his typically pale face was painted in crimson and a flush of pink. Simply... Perfect

Even though Chikashi was completely aware of what was happening and understood how genuine and innocent his sentiments were, he was unable to accept them. After all that had occurred the previous day, it may have just been a moment of confusion. Why did this need to occur? This morning, everything was easy and nice, until...

"Shuuji..." He said, "I don't think," to start.

"Shuu! Chikashi! Kurokawa-kun is eager to talk to you!" Chikashi's words were cut short as Shun shouted out to the two. Sighing, he got to his feet. "Let's go on." This might wait till later. However, he ought to check out what the vice President's agenda is right now.

What the f*ck

Kurokawa was seated there when we knocked on the door of the room. I've been expecting you, he said as he swiveled his chair and grinned at us.

Shuuji glanced aside, ashamed because he recognized this individual, while Shun facepalmed and I just moaned.

Without even noticing, Kurokawa leaned forward and put his hands on the table. To apologize for that other day, I called you two here, I said. Oh. I didn't anticipate an apology from him... Wait! What was wrong with making an apology?

"I hope you won't take it that way, Oikawa-kun. Still, I am. Sorry again. We couldn't have made it work between us." Ah my God! Don't get me wrong, I enjoyed the movie Pirates of the Caribbean. Still do.

After rolling my eyes at what he said, I cast a quick peek at the raven head next to me. It was lovely how joyful he appeared to be. Strangely, he was so cute that I couldn't take my eyes off him. It was irritating, aggravating, and, um, cute.

I don't know what to do with this cute individual. using his endearing smile. If that's all, I'm returning. I then made my way to the door to depart. I catch a glimpse of Shuuji bowing slightly and almost running after me. I sigh. At least that was finished and put to rest.

Now, about this issue...

"Chikashi!"

"What's that?" I complained while furrowing my brow.

Please give me some thoughts.

Already carrying it out.

"I'm returning to class," you said. He murmured, his cheeks blushing. It must have required an enormous amount of guts... He made me giggle because I recognized myself in him. Ah, I'm not going to allow him to commit the same errors. I was unable. He may have appeared menacing and tall, but whatever. He is kind, cute, wonderful, and priceless. To me, he was incredibly significant.

For his sake, I had to let him go.

I still required bravery, though.

xxxxxxxxxxxx

I threw off my shoes and dragged my feet over to the couch, where I flopped down and moaned. Today was quite exhausting.

After welcoming us and locking the door, Shun motioned for me to sit up and sat down next to me. "Room?"

Knowing what he was about to say, I nodded in agreement. I picked up my luggage and went upstairs, leaving my brother in my wake.

When he noticed the little disarray in my room, dad sat on my bed and sighed, saying, "You really should keep your things."

"Maybe. However, why not tomorrow?" I chimed as I took my uniform off and unbuttoned it. What happened to the topic you intended to discuss with me, then?

I stood in front of my bed that came just below my knees, leaped a little, and fell into the plush mattress as Shun spoke. He coughed, then sat up as he said, "So... I heard about Shuuji-confession." kun's

Yes, I complained, "I know I know, you ought to give it a shot." I slightly over-emphasized my brother's voice as I mimicked it. It's not like I didn't comprehend his emotions. I just...

"You really ought to! What happened to the other one, specifically?" Shun turned to face me with his brows wrinkled.

"Clingy."

"Well—"

"He once attempted to stab me."

"What?!" Shun coughed.

I shattered his arm.

He said nothing.

I also did. I'm confident that he was aware of my fear. I sighed and hid my face in my warm blanket. After a brief delay, the door opened as I heard it close. I sighed and turned to face the visitor before sitting up right away. As I did so, my hand slipped off the cover as I tried to secure it, and I felt the mattress on my back, which seemed as though it were knocking the air out of me.

With his hands near to my head, Shuuji cast a shadow over me. He appeared agitated, but he also gave off the impression of being definite and knowing exactly what he intended to accomplish, albeit with some uncertainty.

"Sh-Shuuji?" I giggled apprehensively while shoving him away with my hands.

My lack of a top makes me exposed, and I doubt I could strike him if I tried. I'm not exactly in a secure position. My hands are already too frail to even touch him, much less hit him. "Chikashi..."

"-kun, kindly don a shirt. If you didn't, I wouldn't be able to restrain myself."

He helped me up and then climbed away from me while holding my hand.

I shivered and took his hand to help me get up while I looked over at him. Except for a slight blush on his cheeks, he appeared in good health.

"Never do that action. I may strike you, "I made a threat.

Shuuji raised irises "It wasn't you. I'm taken aback."

An absolute llama!

"I simply didn't want to hurt you," I said. Oh, sh*t, I stumbled. Half the truth is not a lie! "Now leave! I desire a bath!"

I shoved him outside and shut the door, I slammed the door shut after attempting to ignore his menacing glare and soothing my tense and racing heart.

I exhaled, gathered my composure, and moved toward the restroom. He had to decide what to do. possess self-control? What threat? I took off my jeans and then my underwear before entering the restroom.

Oh.

Whether it was the heat of the water or whatever I was thinking, I felt my cheeks flush. I cleaned my face in panic and came dangerously close to drowning.

Imagine, though, that Shuuji was to wretch on top of me. or under... Oh my God, the look on his face as he penetrates me hard and experiences ecstasy... His grimace, oh!

Wow, fuck me.

I rapidly dispelled such ideas before getting more ecstatic and, well,

After rinsing the shampoo from my hair, I turned off the faucet and dried myself with a towel.

I exited my room wearing a basic T and a pair of trousers with the towel still dangling from my shoulders.

What will we be eating?

Shuuji's cuisine Shuuji was in the kitchen while Shun was sort of tidying the living room. I approached Shuuji and took a seat next to him to observe him at work.

"Chikashi... Please don't remain still. It's quite annoying."

What did he mean by distracting, I scowled.

Maybe if you spoke what you wanted to do to him aloud, he would understand. The sound of Shun's voice reached our ears.

Shuuji took a swallow and began mumbling, "I want to hold you up against the table and mark you all over. I'll take off your clothes after that and-"

I struck him on the head a bit softer than I had meant, but he still cried out in pain.

I've got it, I've got it! Why the hell are you blushing? I exhaled deeply as I delicately patted my cheeks. Shuu-chan Chikashi-nii declared that he preferred you to Kurokawa-Kun for a date.

She told Shuuji what I said that day when I swung around and heard the tiny demon laughing at me. After some time of stillness, Shuuji knelt and stroked Yumi's head "Exactly so? Please persuade him to accompany me on a date. Than anyone else, I would rather date Chikashi-Kun."

I raced up to my room right away, shaking with anxiety. How could he be that slick? He's so-!

I sank into my bed and curled up under my cover, refusing to think anything while I lay there. "Chikashi! It's mealtime!"

I moaned and rose off the bed.

xxxxxx

I had no idea why Shuuji was in my room, and I questioned if it would be a good cause. Shun had gone to a friend's house to study because exams were approaching. He also gave me the address, and I watched him go with apprehension.

I flipped over the pages of my book while staring at it, unable to take in anything as my eyes skimmed the passing words. I shifted uneasily in my seat as Shuuji, who was seated across from me, gave me a sidelong glance.

We briefly locked eyes.

I won't suddenly jump you or anything, I promise.

I wasn't thinking about what she said.

It was.

With a glance, Shuuji appeared to be able to see straight through me. I object to that. Uncomfortably shifting in my seat, I let my attention drift to the book on the table, reading the passages but once more learning nothing.

"Chikashi... I like you, and I..."

"I understand,"

Again, Shuuji ceased speaking. I moaned as my chest constricted. Why him out of all the handsome, good-looking lads in the world?

I was at a loss for what to do. He liked me, but I was hindered by my dread. He was heterosexual, I suppose, and I honestly don't know what to say. Despite wanting to be at his side...

I took a deep breath and stood up. I moved toward the raven's head and knelt in front of him. I then pushed him down and put my hands next to his head, pushing in closer so that, unlike my sexuality, I could stare directly into his eyes.

What are you now experiencing?

Shuuji sucked in.

I grinned. I got the precise response I needed. I took a deep breath to relax, then I silently heard my heartbeat. In addition to the fuzzy feeling I had, it was moving at a somewhat accelerated pace. I was also confident in myself.

Shuu, I like you too.

While Shuuji pursed his lips and threw his arms around my neck, there was a look of delight in his eyes. His lips touched mine as I leaned forward.

Something warm and moist found its way into my mouth. My body jolted, sending tingles across all of my senses, and I instantly felt dizzy. How was this youngster so skilled at KISSING?

My palm tucked my fingers into it. My head was foggy from the kiss and his tongue searching my mouth as I withdrew, panting for oxygen. You're meant to be bad at this, right? I looked aside and mumbled somewhat fiercely.

"Chikashi, I'm not a virgin."

I laughed while trying to hide my amazement and, um, envy.

My back was forced to collapse as a result of Shuuji pushing me and turning me to the side while holding onto my shoulders. We traded places.

I swallowed. His eyes were locked on mine and were obscured by something I don't often see. Lust.

Shuuji leaned in and encircled me with his hands. I steadied my breath as I got ready for another kiss.

I was certain he liked me as I peered into his eyes. Overwhelmed with passion, tears grew and spilled from the side of my eyes...

I enjoy him. I enjoy him. I enjoy him. I enjoy him.

I adore this guy.

Once more, our lips touched, and I reached up to touch his head, sliding my fingers through his hair to feel it. It was supple. Very smooth and soft.

"Chikashiiiiii!!!!"

Hearing my name made my body tense, and I immediately shoved Shuuji away, earning a shocked expression from him. I stood up and stared at the door. It blasted open with a loud "BAM," and my old pal was standing there. Tanami Jin, the one and only, was ecstatic.

Keep going as you are

We just had to be interrupted when things were going well.

When Jin first saw me, he smiled, but when he noticed Yuuta standing next to me, he scowled. He flipped his fringe to the point where it reached his eyebrows and then inspected Yuuta from top to bottom. Jin had the look of someone who was contemplating with pursed lips. His royal blue jacket was so large that it barely revealed his attractive form as he crossed his arms across his chest. The garment also covered his arms.

His curious gaze and little sense of uneasiness with the stranger in front of him gave him a childlike appearance. He had a talent for beguiling, and even though the last time I saw him was while he was sobbing, he was still as calm and endearing as before. I couldn't take my eyes off of him.

What I would anticipate from my first love. Jin was my senior on the volleyball team and is 19 years old, making him 2 years older than us. I confessed to him on the day of his graduation, but he rejected me right away, grinning and apologizing, and claiming that he was seeing Kurokawa Yuuji, the brother of the one and only Kurokawa Senji, who was going out with someone else. Even so, we became friends. After I finally moved on from him, I developed feelings for the nerd sitting next to me.

Jin approached Yuuta and knelt before extending his hand and saying, "Hello," to the man who, like me, couldn't take his eyes off of him "Jin Tanami. Pleasant to meet you."

I could guess that Yuuta had made this guy his master right away based on the little flush and admiration in his eyes. Jin was held in Yuuta's hand as he introduced himself and said his name as if he were a lost dog who had found his owner. Jin exuded a strong sense of brotherliness, which is why practically everyone is moved by both his youthfulness and, when necessary, his maturity. It was also the reason he was only able to date those who entered my room.

No matter how one looked at him, Kurokawa Yuuji seemed to be the elder brother everyone wanted. However, Jin claimed that if one got to know him better, he would be uncomfortable and seldom take the initiative to accomplish something. He provided Jin with all she needed. Jin wanted someone he could protect and also someone who would protect him because he was the older brother and occasionally needed to be showered with affection. Yuuji was that person, and occasionally, just occasionally, I wished I was just like Yuuji. In a sense, he made me envious.

Jin went up to me after shaking hands with Yuuta. He slipped a little bit, yelping cutely, but he soon caught himself and hugged me. "Chikashiii, you were missed!"

I give him a pat on the back and say, "I missed you too." Because he smelled like books, I immediately assumed that he had either gone to a library and hit a book-stacked object by accident, causing the books to fall on him, or that he had simply gone to a bookstore and spent hours looking through books there.

It seemed like Yuuta was moping a little to me when I heard Yuuji sigh. Shun was at home when Yuuji drew Jin away from me and apologized for the intrusion.

I felt like I was meeting my parents as I sat next to Yuuta and across from Yuuji and Jin, Jin's eyebrows slightly wrinkled in the center. The brunette drank nervously on his hot tea while scorching his lips in the process.

Jin exclaimed, "Ow-Ow- Hot-," and hurriedly set his cup of tea down on the table. Quickly responding, Yuuji raised the other man's chin gently so that Jin was facing him. He then leaned in and softly stroked his tongue over Jin's lips.

As I saw this, I mentally swore and turned my head away as the person next to me swiftly diverted his attention, his cheeks sporting a little scarlet tint.

I turned to look at the pair and noticed Yuuji's thumb delicately resting on his lips and Jin's gorgeous red-flushed ears. "Is that better?" I said.

IS THAT SOME KIND OF SHIT CORNY LINE?

I resisted the urge to chuckle and did my best not to glance at the two. Shun was hiding behind the counter, presumably blushing profusely since she was used to such displays of emotion, especially amongst a couple that included two men. I noticed this out of the corner of my right eye.

So, you two are dating, I take it?" Jin said as he leaned over to us with a small ashamed expression on his face. He told us.

Although Yuuta and I had confessed but hadn't asked each other out just yet, Jin had already determined that we were, "You like each other right?" Jin questioned.

Jin shrugged and said, "Then it's settled," as we both nodded.

"Ah, I wished Chikashi and I had more time together. But I suppose this just means Yuuji and I will have more free time." After sounding sad at the concept, Jin chimed. He'd always been an upbeat person.

Jin gave his cup of tea a little blow, then drank the entire thing while gently exhaling to reduce the heat. When getting up and thanking Shun for the cup of tea, he finally left after Yuuji finished his. When they were about to depart, Jin spoke to the door.

"I apologize for upsetting that flow right now. I'll bet it was the ideal setting for "that." But watch it, okay, since you both are still minors."

I recalled that he was adept at gauging the setting and mood as well, but I wasn't aware of how excellent he was at it until he gave me an embarrassment-inducing wink.

After they departed, I sighed and shut the door. I then turned to look at Yuuta, who appeared to be feeling similarly relieved. Jin was like an idol to me, yet he occasionally made me feel uneasy since it seemed like he could read me like a book. Shun was exhausted from what had just transpired and was upstairs in his room.

Although it didn't seem perfect and there were a lot of things we could have done better, I believe we could have done better because the future is so far away. The one thing we cannot do, however, remains in our current position.

THE END

www.ingramcontent.com/pod-product-compliance
Lightning Source LLC
LaVergne TN
LVHW052054160826
845678LV00015B/3214

* 9 7 9 8 8 4 7 9 2 2 1 9 7 *